Thank you Paul!! :)

☐ YOU'RE SPECIAL   ☐ I LIKE YOU JUST THE WAY YOU ARE
☐ WOULD YOU BE MINE?   ☐ COULD YOU BE MINE?

Thank you for the tickets this year! Thank you for the opportunity you gave Mike! And for fun times at OM!

NEIGHBORHOOD TROLLEY

Maew's Home Journey

By Rose Bruno Bailey

Illustrated By Nerissa Tony

To the compassionate rescuers of all animals without a voice. Thank you for all the good you do. Together we share unconditional love.

- R.B.B.

This is dedicated to God, my daughter, my boo, and my family.

- N.T.

MacLaren-Cochrane Publishing, Inc.

Text©2021 Rose Bruno Bailey
Cover and Interior Art©2021 Nerissa Tony

Maew's Home Journey Dyslexic Edition

For information, e-mail the publisher at:

MCPInfo@Maclaren-Cochranepublishing.com

Library of Congress Control Number: 2021935776

First Edition

ISBN
Hardcover: 978-1-64372-430-0
Softcover: 978-1-64372-431-7

For orders, visit

www.MCP-Store.com
www.maclaren-cochranepublishing.com
www.facebook.com/maclaren-cochranepublishing

Maew is a beautiful Siamese cat with a graceful walk and bi
blue eyes that sparkle. Maew's full name is Maew Kar Deinthang;
a grand name for a grand looking cat. Despite the fancy name and
big blue eyes, Maew comes from very humble beginnings.

He doesn't even know how to say his own
name, so he introduces himself as Meow. It's
spelled Maew, but to everyone he meets he's
just Meow, another stray cat living under a tree
behind a Thai restaurant in Pittsburgh, PA.

Maew longs to curl up on his very own cushion next to a warm fireplace, as he falls asleep smelling the scents of a real home cooked meal. He wants a place where he fits in. What Maew wants more than anything is a forever house.

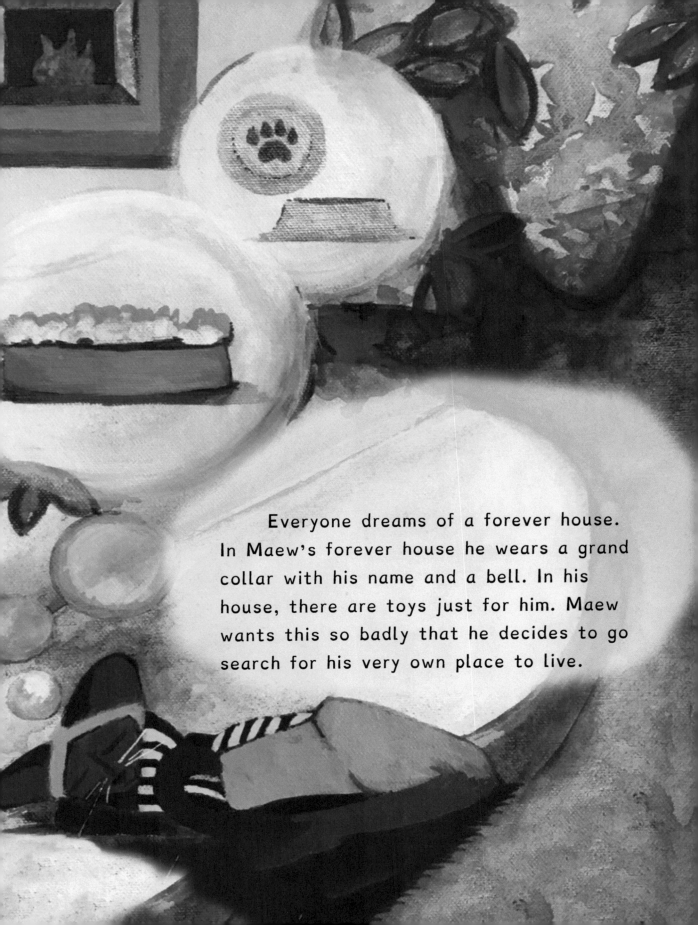

Everyone dreams of a forever house. In Maew's forever house he wears a grand collar with his name and a bell. In his house, there are toys just for him. Maew wants this so badly that he decides to go search for his very own place to live.

Maew takes a leap and leaves the only home he's ever known, the tree behind the Thai restaurant. It's a risk because there are always scraps of food available to eat and the humans are kind. Soon fall will arrive, and with that, so will the cold weather.

Maew knows that now is the time
to find his forever house. He meows goodbye to
this place where he grew up since when he was a
kitten. This was the place where he was named
Maew Kar Deinthang.

Maew first sees a giant oak tree, so he decides to climb it to see if the tree can be his forever house.

Inside the center of the tree is a giant birdhouse with birds of every shape and color. The birds are friendly and chirp to Maew to stay. Maew cannot fly so instead he decides to thank them and continue his search for his forever house.

Next Maew walks by the Ohio River, where friendly happy fish live. The fish float to the surface and splash Maew playfully. When they learn he's looking for a forever house, they invite him to come to the bottom of the river where they live in a sunken abandoned boat.

Maew doesn't swim, so he thanks the fish and again moves on.
e starts to lose hope that he will ever find his forever house.

Soon it starts to rain, with thunder and lightning. Maew crawls into the bushes for shelter and starts to cry. He cries loud meows as his dream is lost, and he's hungry and lonely.

Maew misses his kind friends from the Thai restaurant and the scraps of food they shared. Maybe he should have stayed with the birds or the fish, even though he doesn't know how to fly or swim. Maew has lost all remaining hope.

Then he hears two ladies singing as they walk in the rain. They stop at a red light, so Maew meows as loud as his raspy Siamese voice can meow, with hope that they can hear him and help. The light changes to green and Maew's heart sinks.

Maew curls up under the bushes and cries himself to sleep. All of a sudden, he is in the arms of one of the nice ladies.

They take Maew to a big house where he lives with his new mommy and daddy. Maew has a cushiony bed by the warm fireplace, a fancy collar with his name and a bell, and food and toys all just for him. Maew has everything he ever dreamed of.

Maew soon discovers they are moving. His mommy and daddy are adventurers. What does this mean and where are they going? Maew is afraid he is not going too, so he cries sad meows. His mommy and daddy reassure him that he'll always be with them on all their travels.

Soon the family of three move away from Pittsburgh to New York City, then to San Francisco, and finally to Hollywood. With his family, Maew has lived in places he has never dreamed about, but he's always had everything he dreamed of.

Maew always has his cushiony bed, a collar with his name and a bell, lots of food to eat, and toys of his very own. He soon realizes he has something more meaningful than the things he thought made up a house.

Maew learns it is not a house that he dreamt of all those years ago, but a home. He learns that in a house it is love that makes it a home. His humans love him like no other, and he loves them.

แมว = Maew; Translation = CAT

In Hollywood, Maew learns something else from his world traveler parents. He learns that his real name, Maew Kar Deinthang, means Cat Happy Journey in Thai. It is a grand name given to a humble Siamese cat by his friends who own the Thai restaurant.

Maew lived out the meaning
of his name, when he went on his
own cat happy journey.

Maew traveled a long distance to find
out he wasn't just searching for a forever
house, but a forever home.

Maew learned it's not
four walls that make a home,
but four loving arms.

In Maew's new home in Hollywood he didn't curl up in his favorite cushiony bed. Instead he slept on the cushiony lap of his loving adoptive mommy. Maew was finally home, forever.

Home is Love

Author

Rose Bruno Bailey

Rose Bruno Bailey is a poet/writer, philanthropist, vegan wellness blogger, and author of "Camellia in Snow." Her work is published online and in print magazines. She was born in Chicago and raised in Cleveland, Ohio. Her background is in the theater with an emphasis on dance. Her life journey has taken her from coast to coast and many places in between. Her partners in this journey are her husband James, two beloved Siamese cats Spanky and Max, and rescue cat Cosmo.

"No child is ever lonely who has a furry friend and a book to curl up with. This book is dedicated to children of all ages and the educators that inspire their curiosity to read.

In reverence to the many cats and dogs who completed our family, past and present. They are the loves of my life.

To the adults and children who love their own animal families, which come in all shapes and sizes. Companion animals can be cats, dogs, or even pigs. Love and loyalty are what make a house a home.

Finally, thanks to: Kristen Sheppard for her inspiration and guidance, Tannya Derby my publisher, Nerissa Tony for her artistic collaboration, Melissa Bender who made this story possible, my dear family, and my loving husband James for his continuous support."

Rose Bruno Bailey

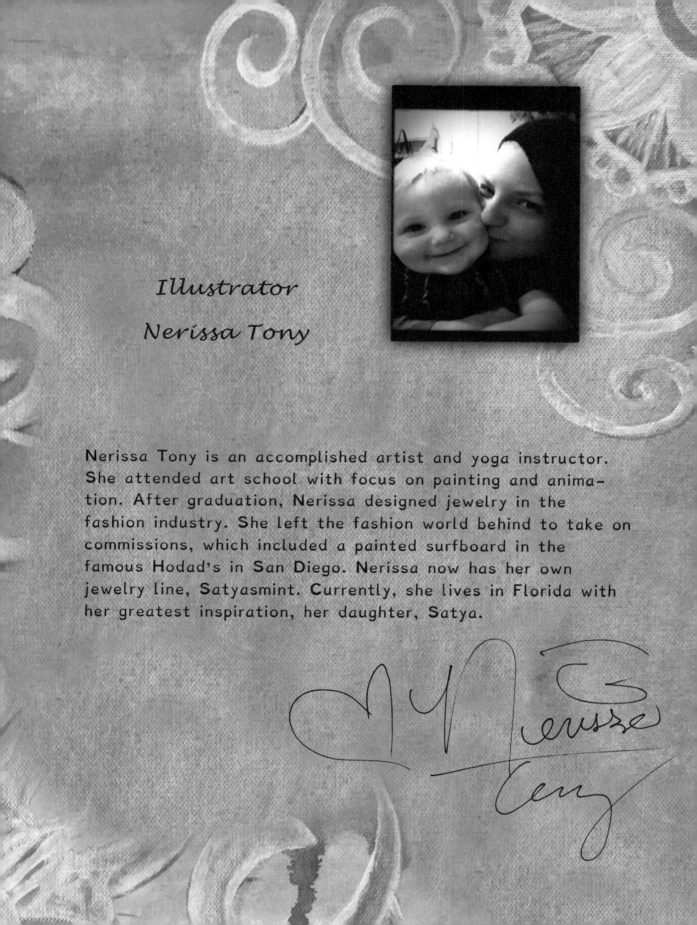

Illustrator

Nerissa Tony

Nerissa Tony is an accomplished artist and yoga instructor. She attended art school with focus on painting and animation. After graduation, Nerissa designed jewelry in the fashion industry. She left the fashion world behind to take on commissions, which included a painted surfboard in the famous Hodad's in San Diego. Nerissa now has her own jewelry line, Satyasmint. Currently, she lives in Florida with her greatest inspiration, her daughter, Satya.

What is Dyslexie Font?

Each letter is given its own identity making it easier for people with dyslexia to be more successful at reading.

The Dyslexie font:
1 Makes letters easier to distinguish
2 Offers more ease, regularity and joy in reading
3 Enables you to read with less effort
4 Gives your self-esteem a boost
5 Can be used anywhere, anytime and on (almost) every device
6 Does not require additional software or programs
7 Offers the simplest and most effective reading support

The Dyslexie font is specially designed for people with dyslexia, in order to make reading easier – and more fun. During the design process, all basic typography rules and standards were ignored. Readability and specific characteristics of dyslexia are used as guidelines for the design.

Graphic designer Christian Boer created a dyslexic-friendly font to make reading easier for people with dyslexia, like himself.

"Traditional fonts are designed solely from an aesthetic point of view," Boer writes on his website, *"which means they often have characteristics that make characters difficult to recognize for people with dyslexia. Oftentimes, the letters of a word are confused, turned around or jumbled up because they look too similar."*

Designed to make reading clearer and more enjoyable for people with dyslexia, Dyslexie uses heavy base lines, alternating stick and tail lengths, larger openings, and semicursive slants to ensure that each character has a unique and more easily recognizable form.

Our books are not just for children to enjoy, they are also for adults who have dyslexia who want the experience of reading to the children in their lives.

Learn more and get the font for your digital devices at www.dyslexiefont.com

Get books in Dyslexie Font at: www.mcp-store.com

5 **I can read to myself**   Complex plots, challenging vocabulary, and high-interest topics for the independent reader.

CPSIA information can be obtained
at www.ICGtesting.com
Printed in the USA
BVHW052159230421
605089BV00005B/9